MARC BROWN

Say Cheese!

Arthur and his friends lined up for the annual Elwood City Bike-a-Thon.

Sue Ellen pointed to the first prize. "That is the coolest camera I have ever seen!"

"There's a lot of competition this year," Buster said.

"I could win this race with my hands tied behind my back," said Francine.

"Better keep them on the handlebars," teased Muffy.

"I'll finish first," said the Brain.

Arthur had never heard the Brain sound so confident.

The horn sounded and Francine took the lead. Arthur and Sue Ellen were close on her tail, but the Brain was far behind.

"So much for finishing first!" called Francine.

No one saw the Brain turn onto a side path.

The Brain opened his backpack and pulled out his invention.
He strapped on his "fantastic" helmet.

"Nothing like a little jet propulsion," said the Brain.

"What took you so long?" asked the Brain.

"How did you get here so fast?" asked Arthur.

"Amazing!" said Sue Ellen.

"You could say that..." The Brain smiled.

"No fair!" said Francine. "You were way behind us!"

"All I did was use my head," said the Brain.

In the next part of the race, everyone rode together until the Brain began to slow down.

"I'm a little tired," he said. "I think I'll stop for a few minutes."

"Are you okay?" asked Arthur.

"Sure," said the Brain. "You go on. I'll catch up."

Once everyone was out of sight, the Brain opened his backpack.

"A little of my go-fast goo on the gears should do the trick," he said.

A few seconds later, he whizzed past Francine.

"He's hardly even pedaling," noticed Arthur.

"Look at him go!" cried Buster.

Francine huffed and puffed trying to keep up.

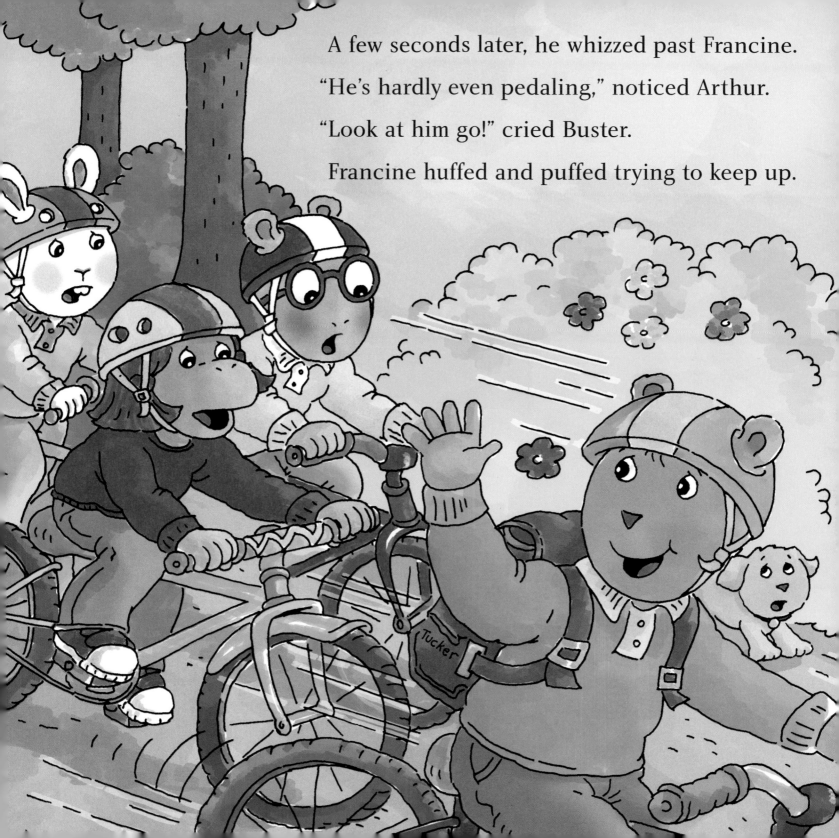

Everyone stopped at the second rest stop. Everyone except the Brain.

Arthur noticed some papers fly out of his backpack as he zoomed by.

"Hey, wait," said Arthur. "You dropped something..."

But it was too late.

Arthur couldn't believe his eyes. "Fantastic helmet? Go-fast goo? Supersonic Trek-tracker? What's going on?"

The last part of the race had lots of twisting paths.

The Brain stopped at a fork in the road.

"Time for a shortcut," he said. "My Supersonic Trek-tracker will find the quickest path."

The device beeped and blinked.

"Let's see," said the Brain. "Two beeps means go left...or is it right?"

But when he reached into his backpack for his plans, they were gone!

"Uh-oh," he said. "I'll have to guess."

He guessed right...which was wrong.

"Whoa!" he cried, bumping along a rocky road. "This is N-N-N-OT W-W-W-HAT I HAD IN MIND!"

He stopped to check his trek-tracker again.

He punched a few buttons.

The device flashed green.

"That means go left...I think," he said. "Well, nothing could be worse than that last road."

So the Brain turned left down another path.

"Ouch!" he cried, pedaling through bushes.

"Yuk!" he said, getting splashed with mud.

The Brain stopped to study his trek-tracker. "One last try," he said. "Don't fail me now..."

His trek-tracker flashed a down arrow.

"That's easy," he said. "DOWN means *down!*"

The Brain headed down the hill very fast. But with all his go-fast goo, he couldn't stop.

"Yikes!" he cried.

"Look!" said Sue Ellen. "There's the Brain!"

"Look at him go!" exclaimed Francine.

"But the finish line is that way," said Buster.

"Help!" shouted the Brain. "I can't stop!"

"I can't watch..." said Arthur.

The Brain landed in the pond with a loud SPLASH!

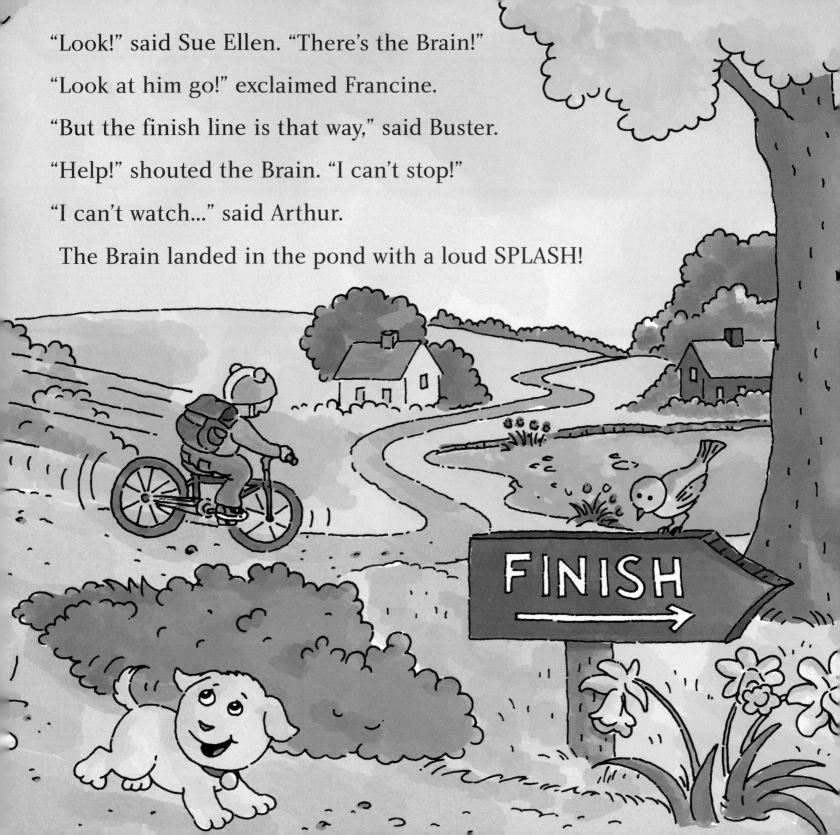

FINISH →

Francine flew across the finish line. "I won!" she hollered.

"I'm second!" called Arthur.

"Third!" cheered Sue Ellen.

Arthur and his friends went back to help the Brain.

"I was just trying to win," said the Brain.

"But what you did wasn't fair," said Francine.

"And you didn't win," added Arthur.

"Don't rub it in," said the Brain.

"Nice camera," said the Brain.

"I just won it," said Francine. "And lucky for you
I'm a good friend. You can borrow it anytime."

"Thanks," said the Brain.

"But I'm taking the first pictures," said Francine.

"Okay, everybody! Say cheese!"